Shoe Bop!

Marilyn Singer

illustrated by Hiroe Nakata

Dutton Children's Books

DUTTON CHILDREN'S BOOKS
A division of Penguin Young Readers Group
Published by the Penguin Group · Penguin Group (USA) Inc.,
375 Hudson Street, New York, New York 10014, U.S.A. · Penguin Group (Canada),
90 Eglinton Avenue East, Suite 700, Toronto, Ontario, Canada M4P 2Y3
(a division of Pearson Penguin Canada Inc.) · Penguin Books Ltd, 80 Strand,
London WC2R 0RL, England · Penguin Ireland, 25 St Stephen's Green, Dublin 2, Ireland (a division of Penguin
Books Ltd) · Penguin Group (Australia), 250 Camberwell Road, Camberwell, Victoria 3124, Australia (a division
of Pearson Australia Group Pty Ltd) · Penguin Books India Pvt Ltd, 11 Community Centre, Panchsheel Park,
New Delhi – 110 017, India · Penguin Group (NZ), 67 Apollo Drive, Rosedale, North Shore 0632, New Zealand
(a division of Pearson New Zealand Ltd) · Penguin Books (South Africa) (Pty) Ltd, 24 Sturdee Avenue, Rosebank,
Johannesburg 2196, South Africa · Penguin Books Ltd, Registered Offices:
80 Strand, London WC2R 0RL, England

Text copyright © 2008 by Marilyn Singer
Illustrations copyright © 2008 by Hiroe Nakata

Library of Congress Cataloging-in-Publication Data

Singer, Marilyn. Shoe bop! / by Marilyn Singer ; illustrations by Hiroe Nakata.—1st ed.
p. cm.
Summary: When her favorite purple tennis shoes fall apart, an
almost-second-grader visits a shoe store, where she tries on footwear of
all colors and styles before finding the pair that is right for her.
ISBN 978-0-525-47939-0
[1. Shoes—Fiction. 2. Shopping—Fiction. 3. Stories in rhyme.]
I. Nakata, Hiroe, ill. II. Title.
PZ8.3.S6154Sho 2008
[E]—dc22   2007028296

Published in the United States by Dutton Children's Books,
a division of Penguin Young Readers Group
345 Hudson Street, New York, New York 10014
www.penguin.com/youngreaders

Designed by IRENE VANDERVOORT

Manufactured in China   First Edition

10 9 8 7 6 5 4 3 2 1

Thanks to Steve Aronson, Lisa Polansky, and my stylish editors, Lucia Monfried and Margaret Woollatt, as well as the whole great Dutton crew.

—MS

For Koharu, who *is* in love with red Mary Janes —HN

Today, my sneakers died.

Purple Sneakers

You purple sneakers, eight months old,
I've loved with all my heart.
We walked, we danced, we ran for miles.
Too bad you fell apart.

Now Mama says, "Aww, don't feel sad.
I've got exciting news.
We'll take the bus, we'll head downtown,
and you can choose new shoes!"

Shoe Bop!

Shoe bop!
I love to shoe shop!
I like to dress my feet
in something new and neat.
Shoe bop!

At the Shoe Store

"What an array!" I hear Mama say.
She means there're lots of shoes on display
for walking and whirling and watching TV,
for enclosing your toes or setting them free,
for riding, for striding, for comfort, for speed.
Which do I want, and which do I need?

What Size Am I?

When the salesman comes to check my size,
he says there's nothing wrong
with a big toe that's not biggest
'cause my second toe's so long.
I nod. I know my toes are fine.
The second one's not scary.
It looks exactly like my dad's
(though his is much more hairy).

The salesman thinks
he's being helpful . . .

Shoe bop!

I love to shoe shop!
I like to check each shelf and
choose those shoes myself.
Shoe bop!

Loafers

"Look," says the salesman,
"each loafer has got,
right there on the front,
a perfect small slot
to put in a penny.
Now, isn't that neat
to walk around twinkling
with coins on your feet?"
He looks so excited,
I won't try to mock it.
But I'm sure I'd prefer
keeping change in my pocket.

Mary Janes

"Try these on—they're Mary Janes."
"What if Mary Jane complains?"
"No, that's what we call these shoes."
"Well, why not Saras? Amys? Sues?
Mary Jane, just who was she?
Why not name shoes after me?"

Saddle Shoes

On the rack, white-and-black
saddle shoes for sale.
Grandma wore them every day
with her swishy ponytail,
a poodle skirt, and little socks.
I love my Gram; I think she rocks.
But I'd leave those shoes inside the box.

SALE

WITHDRAWN

But I don't want school shoes.
It's sneakers I need . . .

Sneakers

Sneakers for basketball,
sneakers for running.
Sneakers with sequins
   that make me look stunning.
Sneakers for gym class
(p.u., how they'll reek).
But where are the sneakers
   to wear when I sneak?

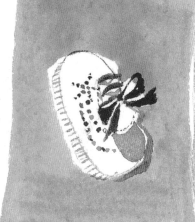

Shoe Rainbow

Turquoise, lime green, apricot,
pink that's pale and pink that's hot.
Striped or dotted, plaid or swirly,
brilliant, boring, ruby, pearly,
lavender, lilac, even plum,
everything but purple.
How dumb!

. . . don't I?

Maybe I should get party shoes instead . . .

Dress-up Shoes

Like candles on a cake,
a piñata and a stick,
a ribbon on a present,
a magician with a trick,

Like everybody singing
"Happy Birthday" all together,
party dresses always go
with shoes of patent leather.

Fancy Sandals

Oh, wouldn't I look grand,
the fairest in the land,
waltzing to the band,
in sandals never meant
for sand!

High Heels

I like how it feels
to wear high heels,
platforms or wedges,
I can peek over hedges.
I can reach a tall shelf.
I'm so proud of myself.
Mama says, "No,
wait till you grow."
But isn't it true
that's what heels
make you *do*?

Hiking Boots

These are travel boots,
dirt and gravel boots,
mountain-climbing boots,
summer-timing boots,
let's go exploring boots,
no time for snoring boots,
we won't be boring boots.
These are rip-roaring boots!

Waders

In the closet with Daddy's suits
are overalls attached to boots.
They're part of his fly-fishing gear.
I really wish they sold them here.
Does anyone make rubber waders
the size for almost-second-graders?

Water Shoes

Mama and I make a fabulous team,
swashing and sloshing our way down a stream.
While Daddy goes fishing, we search for bright stones
or perch on the boulders as if they were thrones.
To keep our feet safe so that they never bruise,
what about buying these rubbery shoes?
I'd get a pair and she'd buy one, too.
Hey, Mr. Crayfish, watch out! Coming through!

shoes that are noisy . . .

Clogs

Clogs, clogs,
   made from logs.
Wooden soles,
   wooden floor.
Two shoes click
   and clack like four!

. . . or shoes that are not.

Moccasins

Walk like a deer, these moccasins say.
You can clomp like a cow any old day.

Rain shoes, sun shoes . . .

Galoshes

On our corner when there's rain,
a pond appears and folks complain.
But with galoshes, high and blue,
that pond's a place to splish-splash through.
These boots and I could have such fun—
except on days with lots of sun.

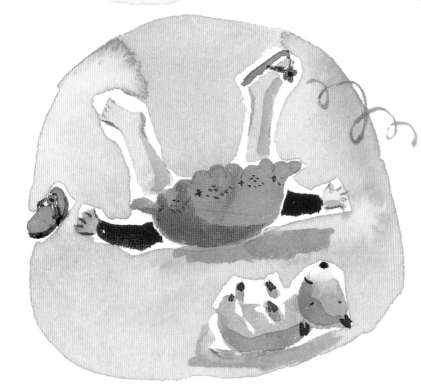

Flip-flops

Flip-flops are tip-top,
but no good to skip, hop.
They kind of go slip-slop,
and then I might trip, plop,
right here in the shoe shop.

Shoes I used to wear . . .

Jellies

Some lady yelled "Elly,
don't bite that jelly!"
And I remembered being two
when I tried to eat my shoe.

T-straps

T-straps?
Perhaps.
Who could forget?
They taught me my first letter
of the alphabet!

Bedroom Slippers

I once had bunny slippers.
Now here's hippo, chimp, giraffe.
Which would I wear to the zoo,
to make those critters laugh?

. . . shoes I've never worn at all!

Cowboy Boots

If I get these boots,
I'll need a swingy skirt,
I'll need a sparkly shirt,
    a cowgirl hat, of course.
If I get these boots,
I'll need a fringy vest,
a saddle from the West.
    I'll need a frisky horse!

WITHDRAWN

Ballet Flats

In ballet flats I stand up tall.
I stretch my neck; I flap my wings.
I might just fly across the mall.
These slippers are such magic things—
the moment that I put them on,
I turned from chicken into swan!

Chinese Slippers

Shoes of leather, shoes of suede,
Here's a pair that looks crocheted.
Those are plastic. These are made
in red and gold and green like jade
from a pretty word:
brocade.

ALL of these shoes?

NONE of these shoes!

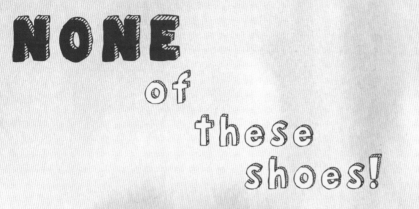

Shoes I'm Not Getting Today

Toe shoes,

snow shoes,

swimming flippers.

White nurse shoes,

matching purse shoes,

winter boots with zippers.

Teeny shoes,

genie shoes,

golf shoes with spikes.

First base shoes,

outer space shoes,

any shoes my brother likes!

I really do like sneakers.

Light-up Shoes

Summer nights I could be dashing
through the schoolyard,
heels flash-flashing
red blink red
on the swings, on the slide.
So you'd always find me when I hide.

High-tops

I've got a question—guess I'll ask it:
In high-tops, could I sink a basket?
Leap up high to catch a ball?
Jump a hurdle, never fall?
In high-tops, could I fly so far,
I'd turn into a shooting star?

All these shoes, all these hues,
but it's sneakers that I choose.
Low-tops and purple are yesterday's news.
High-tops are my tops—and the color?

chartreuse!